The PIED PIPER of HAMELIN

Retold by Kay Brown
from the poem by Robert Browning
Illustrated by Gerry Embleton

The town of Hamelin in Northern Germany is famous today because of something which happened there hundreds of years ago. The city is on the banks of the River Weser and was, even then, a large, busy place with many fine buildings.

But Hamelin was a terrible place to live, for one reason –RATS!!

The town was overrun by huge, fearless rats: they attacked the dogs and cats and bit the children in their beds. These rats didn't hide until darkness fell before they searched for food. Oh no, these rats swarmed everywhere all day long, jumped onto tables, and gnawed at the food in the kitchens while it was being cooked! The noise of their squeaking and screaming filled the streets, but whatever the people of Hamelin tried to do to get rid of the rats seemed to have no effect.

At last the townspeople could stand it no longer. They stormed into the Town Hall and confronted the Mayor. "What are you doing about the rats?" they shouted angrily. "Or do you spend all day sitting in fine clothes eating fine lunches – which *we* pay for – while the rest of us suffer? Something *must* be done!"

The Mayor and Councillors were not a little afraid of the shouting crowds and certainly didn't want to lose their fur-trimmed robes of office or the seven-course dinners they enjoyed from time to time! "Surely someone can think of something," wailed the Mayor. "Let's send the town-crier into every square in the city to ask for good ideas, offer a reward perhaps . . . " So the very next day a messenger was heard in every part of Hamelin reading the Mayor's proposal to the crowds:

"THERE WILL BE A REWARD OF ONE THOUSAND GOLD COINS FOR WHOEVER CAN RID THE TOWN OF ITS PLAGUE OF RATS."

Well, of course everyone *had* been trying to think of a
way to get rid of the rats, but they tried even harder on
hearing about the reward. Engineers designed huge traps to
catch the pests; chemists sat up all night trying to find a
poison strong enough to kill them without killing all the

people too. Hunters talked about organising an army to shoot them one by one – and someone even suggested that everyone should leave the city and let the rats stay!
But no one, it seemed, had an idea which would work.

With every day that passed the rats seemed to grow in size and number, and the people grew more desperate.

One morning, during a Council meeting, the doors burst open and there stood a tall, thin stranger. He was dressed in most peculiar clothes of brightest red and yellow; his tunic had long draped sleeves, there was a jaunty feather in his wide-brimmed hat and around his neck on a long cord was a strange pipe.

He smiled mysteriously at the startled Mayor.

In a soft voice, and very politely, he said, "Your honours, I have come halfway round the world to solve your problem. I have been of service to Kings in the West and Sultans in the East and by means of a secret charm I am here in Hamelin to rid you of your rats and claim the reward!"

The Mayor and all the Councillors welcomed him warmly – it seemed as though their prayers had been answered at last. Promising him whatever he wished they urged the stranger to begin his magic at once.

He stepped out into the street and raised the strange pipe to his lips. With eyes twinkling the piper played three high-pitched notes and waited. Far away there was a muttering, mumbling sound; gradually it grew louder like thunder rolling in from the hills. Suddenly, from every house and hole, from every shop and cellar, the rats appeared – old rats, young rats, big rats, small rats, rats of every colour and description. Whatever magic was in the piper's call, the rats were following him as though their lives depended on it.

Through the narrow streets and across the squares the piper danced, playing his shrill notes – and the little creatures followed. More joined the throng at every corner, until it seemed the cobbles were alive with a squealing sea of rats. The townspeople stared from their windows – they couldn't believe what they saw! Who was the prancing stranger dressed in such odd and colourful clothes? What was the magic of his music that no rat could ignore it, but was compelled to scramble and scurry after him across the streets of Hamelin?

On and on the piper sped, right across the city, never tiring, until dusk was falling and he came to the banks of the River Weser.

But the piper played on, wading into the dark water.
After him came the rats! They rushed to the river's edge
and desperately, blindly, hurled themselves after the
stranger. For several hours more the pipe was heard and
well into the night the splashing and squealing
continued . . . until, at last, every rat was drowned.

Next day, when the people of Hamelin realised that the rats had really gone, there was rejoicing in every part of the town. Free from the pests which had plagued their lives, night and day, for as long as anyone could remember! Men, women and children danced and sang in the streets. There was feasting and music and laughter everywhere. "Hurrah for the piper, the Pied Piper of Hamelin!" the happy people cried.

But in the Town Hall, where the piper had gone to collect his money, no one appeared at all grateful.

Having watched the rats drowning in the river the night before, the Mayor felt quite safe in paying the piper not more than one gold coin – instead of the thousand he had promised.

The stranger listened in silence to the Mayor, then his face darkened and he shook with anger. Saying not one word he raced from the room, up the stone steps and onto the roof of the Town Hall. As he stood angrily shaking his fists over the city the skies clouded over and a cold wind began to blow.

The piper stepped down into the street and once more lifted his pipe to his lips. He blew three long, clear notes – then waited and listened.

Faces appeared at doors and windows; women stopped their chattering and men straightened from their work. What was the stranger doing now? Why was he still playing his magic pipe now that all the rats were gone?

Then the children, in two's and three's, came out from their houses, laughing and chattering. At first they came slowly, as if they weren't sure where they were going or why, but the piper began his music again and moved off down the street. Little feet began to run, more children came to join the first, clapping their hands and skipping. When the piper turned the corner the children followed, and the sound of their happy laughter mingled with the music.

As he had done the day before, the piper danced and played his way across Hamelin, through every lane and across every square. Everywhere he passed his sweet music brought out more children to join the chattering crowd at his heels: they joined hands and ran after him without once looking back.

They passed the Town Hall once more, where the Mayor and Councillors stood dumbstruck, unable to move or cry out, and on by the old cathedral at the edge of the city.

By now hundreds were following the piper – every child who was old enough to walk was there – and all were with him as he turned towards the River Weser where the rats had perished.

Just as the horrified
onlookers felt sure their children
were going to drown as the rats had
done, the piper turned to the West, towards a great hill which
looked down on Hamelin. "Thank goodness," the people thought
with great relief, "they'll never be able to cross Koppelberg Hill.
The piper will have to stop, and our children too."